HOW TO DRAW
CARTOONS
AND CARICATURES

Judy Tatchell

Designed by Graham Round

Illustrated by Graham Round, Terry Bave, Robert Walster and Chris Lyon

Additional designs by Brian Robertson and Camilla Luff

Contents

Consultants: Terry and Shiela Bave

About this book

Caricature

Cartoons look quick and easy to draw. You may have found that they are not as easy as they look, though. This book is full of simple ways to do good cartoons.

The first part tells you how to draw cartoon people using simple shapes and lines. You can find out how to draw expressions and movement, too.

A caricature is a funny picture of a real person. You exaggerate things, such as the shape of their nose or hair. You can find out how to do this on pages 8-9.

A comic book.

YAP!

A strip cartoon is a series of pictures which tell a joke or funny short story. You can find out how to build up your own strip cartoons on pages 24-25.

Looking at a comic book is a bit like watching a film and reading a book at the same time. You can see how the Tintin stories were created on pages 30-31.

On pages 34-37, you can find out how cartoon films are made. This is called animation, which means "the giving of life". Cartoons are brought to life in a film.

2

First faces

This page shows you an easy way to draw cartoon faces. All you need is a pencil and a sheet of paper. If you want to color the faces in, you can use crayons or felt tip pens.

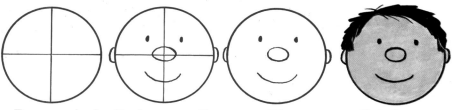

Draw a circle. Do two pencil lines crossing it. Put the nose where the lines cross. The ears are level with the nose. The eyes go slightly above the nose. Erase the lines crossing the face. Add any sort of hair you like.

Faces to copy

Here are some more faces for you to copy. You can see how in a cartoon some things are exaggerated, such as the size of the nose or the expression.

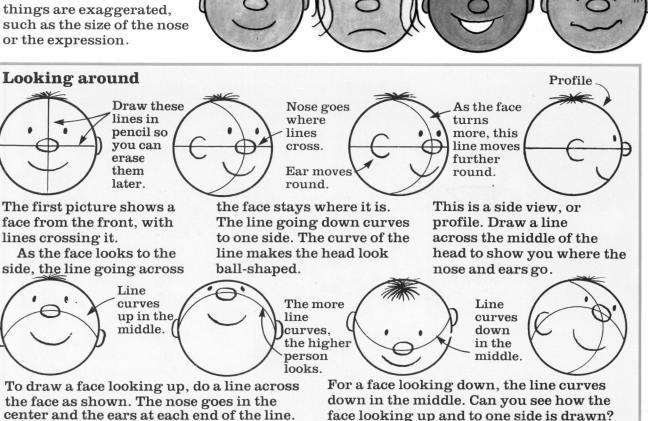

Looking around

Draw these lines in pencil so you can erase them later.

Nose goes where lines cross.

Ear moves round.

As the face turns more, this line moves further round.

Profile

The first picture shows a face from the front, with lines crossing it.

As the face looks to the side, the line going across the face stays where it is. The line going down curves to one side. The curve of the line makes the head look ball-shaped.

This is a side view, or profile. Draw a line across the middle of the head to show you where the nose and ears go.

Line curves up in the middle.

The more line curves, the higher person looks.

Line curves down in the middle.

To draw a face looking up, do a line across the face as shown. The nose goes in the center and the ears at each end of the line.

For a face looking down, the line curves down in the middle. Can you see how the face looking up and to one side is drawn?

Cartoon people

Now you can try adding some bodies to your cartoon faces. There are two different methods described on these pages. The first uses stick figures. The second uses rounded shapes. Try them both and see which you find easier.

Stick figures

Use a pencil, so you can erase the lines later.

Body stick

Keep this line short or the figure will end up bottom-heavy.

Erase a bit of the head line here, where the hair falls forward.

Draw this stick figure. The body stick is slightly longer than the head. The legs are slightly longer than the body. The arms are a little shorter than the legs.

Here are the outlines of some clothes for the figure. You can copy a sweatshirt with jeans or with a skirt. You could also try some dungarees or a dress.

To dress your stick figure, draw the clothes round it, starting at the neck and working down.

You can add long, short, curly or straight hair.

Drawing hands and feet

When someone is facing you, you can see their thumbs and first fingers.

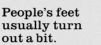

People's feet usually turn out a bit.

Cartoon hands and shoes, like cartoon heads, are larger than on a real person. Practice drawing these shapes before you add them to the figures.

Coloring in

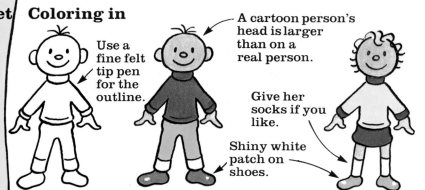

Use a fine felt tip pen for the outline.

A cartoon person's head is larger than on a real person.

Give her socks if you like.

Shiny white patch on shoes.

When you have finished the outline of the figure, go over it with a felt tip pen. When it is dry you can erase the stick figure and color the cartoon in.

The girl needs some lines for legs before you can put on her shoes. When you color the shoes, leave a small, white patch on the toes to make them shiny.

Figures using rounded shapes

The arms are a bit shorter than the body, the legs longer.

Oval body shape

Smoothed-off join.

These stripes are slightly curved to show the rounded shape of the body.

With a pencil, draw a head shape. Add an oval for the body shape and sausages for the arms and legs. The body is about one and a half times as long as the head.

Add the outlines of the clothes, smoothing off any joins, such as between the arms or legs and the body. Go over the outline in ink and erase pencil lines.

Add hands and feet and color the figure in.

You can find out how to make your cartoon figure look as if it is moving on pages 12-15.

More cartoon people to draw

Try varying your rounded shapes or stick figures to draw different-shaped cartoon people.

Tiny person. Head larger in proportion to body.

Tall person. Egg-shaped head and longer body.

Fat person. Head squashed and legs shorter.

Short person. Head, body and legs the same length.

Some things to try

When you have practiced drawing several figures using the methods shown above, you could try drawing a figure outline straight off. If you find it difficult, you can go back to drawing a stick or rounded shape figure first.

Try drawing these different people:
- A fat lady in a fur coat and hat.
- A man with hairy legs in shorts.
- A boy and a girl wearing party clothes.

Making faces

You can make cartoon characters come to life by giving them different expressions. These two pages show you how to do this, by adding or changing a few lines. First, try the faces in pencil. Then you can color them in.

Happy faces

Girls and women tend to have slightly smaller noses than boys and men.

These lines make the ears look more real.

Happiness is shown by a smiling mouth. Drawing the eyes as shown above gives a cheerful expression.

You can make the person burst out laughing by opening the mouth more and showing the teeth.

This is a bigger laugh. The head is thrown back. You can find out how to position the features on page 3.

Sad and angry faces

Sadness and anger are also mainly shown in the eyes and mouth.

Lines show shaking with fury.

Sad: the mouth and eyebrows droop.

Angry: use straight lines for the mouth and eyebrows.

Furious: the person frowns and goes red in the face.

Hopping mad: the mouth is wide open in a loud yell.

More expressions

Here are lots more expressions for you to copy and practice

Winking. Mouth tilts up on side where eye is closed.

Sly. Eyes look sideways and mouth is pursed.

Sickly. Face has a greenish tinge. Tongue hangs out. Eyes are creased up.

White stripes in hair make it look shiny.

Thoughtful. Eyes look up and sideways.

Smug. Sideways grin and half-closed eyes.

You can make the face look fatter by adding curves on the cheeks and chin.

Yawning. Nose squashes up to eyes which are closed. Mouth is wide open showing teeth.

Frightened. Face is pale and bluish. Hair stands on end. Eyes are wide open.

A wavy line for the mouth and droopy eyes give a bored look.

This view of someone is called a three-quarter profile.

Frowning forehead and drooping mouth look worried.

A white patch on the balloon makes it shiny.

Try drawing some of these expressions from different angles. See page 3 if you need help with positioning the features on the face.

Blowing up a balloon. Cheeks are full and eyes closed.

These lines make it look as if the balloon is getting bigger.

Drawing caricatures

A caricature is a picture of someone which exaggerates their most striking or unusual features. Although a caricature looks funny, you can recognize the person easily.

It helps to look at the person, or at a photograph of them, while you are drawing.

Caricatured features

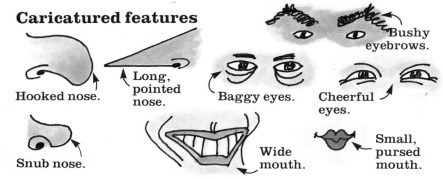

Hooked nose.

Long, pointed nose.

Baggy eyes.

Cheerful eyes.

Bushy eyebrows.

Snub nose.

Wide mouth.

Small, pursed mouth.

Here are some examples of caricatured features. You can copy or adapt them for your own caricatures.

Tricks of the trade

Imagine the features you would pick out if you were describing the person to someone else. These are the features to exaggerate.

Here are some caricatures drawn from photographs. Try copying them.

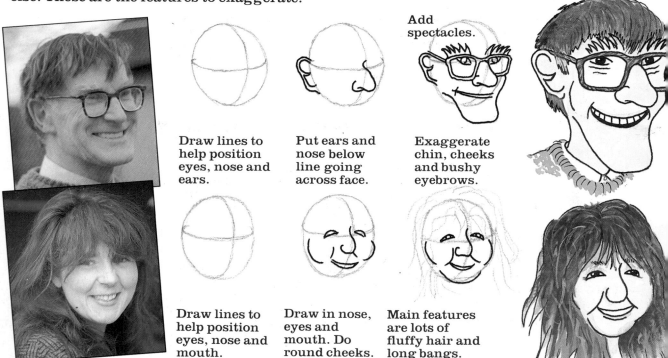

Add spectacles.

Draw lines to help position eyes, nose and ears.

Put ears and nose below line going across face.

Exaggerate chin, cheeks and bushy eyebrows.

Draw lines to help position eyes, nose and mouth.

Draw in nose, eyes and mouth. Do round cheeks.

Main features are lots of fluffy hair and long bangs.

Draw a face shape and lines. Add ear and earring.

Do small, turned-up nose, glasses, and mouth.

Main features are cheeks, spiky hair and glasses.

Head is long and wedge-shaped rather than round.

Draw in a long nose, a smile, an ear and eyes.

Main features are cheeks, long chin and fluffy hair.

Round head. Lines show where eyes and nose go.

Draw a big nose, a grin, eyes and chubby cheeks.

Make chin a bit longer. Do long bangs over eyes.

Caricature yourself

You can draw a funny caricature of yourself by looking at yourself in a shiny spoon. The curve of the spoon distorts your features.

If you look in the back of the spoon, your nose looks very big.

Turn the spoon sideways to get a different effect.

Drawing from different sides

Here you can find out how to draw people from the side and from the back as well as from the front.

You can also see how to make your pictures look interesting by drawing, say, a bird's eye view. There are some instructions for how to do this on the opposite page.

Turning round

Right arm overlaps body.

Right leg overlaps left.

Feet face same way.

As a person begins to turn round, their body gets narrower. (See page 3 for how to draw the face.)

Side view

Arm towards back of body.

Back of hand.

Left leg just visible behind right.

Shape of nose

From the side, the body is at its narrowest. You can see the shape of the nose and the back of one hand.

Back view

You can see the backs of the heels.

From the back, the body parts are the same sizes and shapes as from the front.

More positions to draw

Here are lots of cartoon people, in all sorts of positions. Copy them and they will help you draw people in other positions, too.

Sitting on the ground.

Piggy-back

On a bicycle.

Sitting on a chair.

Drawing a bird's eye view

A bird's eye view can make an ordinary picture look quite dramatic. Try drawing this group.

The parts of the body nearer to you are bigger than those further away. Also, the bodies are shorter than if you were drawing them from straight on. This is called foreshortening.

Draw a set of pencil lines fanning out from a point. Fit the people roughly in between them.

Heads look biggest as they are nearest.

Pencil lines help get the proportions of the people right.

Bodies get smaller the further away they are.

A worm's eye view

Bodies get smaller the further away they are and they are foreshortened.

A worm's eye view is from ground level. Draw another set of pencil lines starting from the top. This time, the people's feet are biggest.

The head of the tallest person is the smallest.

Looking from the bottom, the feet are biggest.

Hints for the pictures

Try to space the lines evenly. This means that all the people will get larger at the same rate.

Big people can slightly overlap the lines, and small people can fall within them.

The longer you draw the people, the more of a worm's eye view the picture will become. This is also true for a bird's eye view.

11

Moving pictures

Here, you can find out how to draw cartoon people walking, running, jumping and so on. Start with a stick or shape figure if it helps.

Walking and running

The right arm is in front when the left leg is forward.

Stick figure to help you get the body right.

Draw the figure just above ground level to show he is on the move.

Add a few curved lines to show fast movement.

Blobs of sweat flying off head.

When someone is walking briskly, they lean forwards slightly. There is always one foot on the ground.

Starting to run, the body leans forwards even more. The elbows bend and move backwards and forwards.

The faster someone is going, the more the body leans forwards and the further the arms stretch.

Jumping

The more this leg bends, the higher the jump will be.

Both feet come forward to hit the ground.

Running towards the jump . . .

Taking off . . .

In mid-flight . . .

Landing from the jump.

Falling over

These pictures show a stick person running along and tripping over. Copy them and then fill in the body shapes around the stick figures.

Action pictures

Here are lots of action pictures to try. There are stick figures next to each picture, to help you get the body right. Look at page 4 if you need reminding how long each part of the body should be.

Diving

Lines show direction of movement.

Hitting

These curved lines show the swing of the racket.

Throwing

These lines show the path of the ball.

Swimming

Add lots of splashes and movement lines.

Rollerskating

Arm stretched out in front.

Rollerskating is similar to running but there is always a foot on the ground.

Skateboarding

Body leaning back and legs bent.

You can get a good sense of turning a corner fast by bending the body and legs.

Kicking

When kicking a ball, the body twists towards the foot that is kicking.

13

More movement

Here are some even more dramatic ways to show movement. You exaggerate certain things to give an impression of lots of speed or effort. You can write words on a picture to give extra impact.

Beads of perspiration.

Fists clenched.

Legs spinning.

Clouds of dust.

You can even add movement lines round the letters.

Make the letters big and bold. You could do them in color.

This is someone running to catch a bus. You can add a word like ZOOM or WHIZZ, with an exclamation mark.

Wheel spin.

The hair and scarf of the skater on the left are streaming out behind her. This gives a sense of speed.

These figures look like they are running away. The dust clouds get smaller as they get further away.* The

figures are in the distance, so they are small. A curved line for the ground gives a feeling of space.

These silhouettes have long shadows to make it look like evening.

*This is called perspective. There is more about it on pages 20-21.

Freeze-frame pictures

You can draw pictures that look frozen in the middle of exciting action, as if you were freezing a video during a film. You do this by adding details of moving things, such as those in the pictures here.

Wide mouth and eyes and spinning head make him look dazed.

Ski pole flying through the air makes it look like the accident has just happened.

Snow swooshing up as skier comes to a sudden halt.

Boy's wallet falling from his pocket.

You could copy this picture, but try drawing different costumes, hairstyles and expressions.

Girl's drink spilling.

An action scene to try

These lines make it look like the person is somersaulting.

Try drawing someone trampolining. They might get into all sorts of positions in the air.

Some freeze-frame ideas

Scenes where there is a lot of action are good for freeze-frame pictures.

You could try an ice-rink, a windy day, or a party by a swimming pool.

Drawing stereotypes

As well as drawing caricatures of real people (see pages 8-9), you can draw caricatures of different types of people, such as a burglar or a chef. These are called stereotypes. They are not pictures of real people but you can recognize from the pictures what sort of people they are or what they do for a living.

You normally recognize a stereotype from the shape of the body and the clothes. Here are some to try.

(see pages 8-9)

Getting started

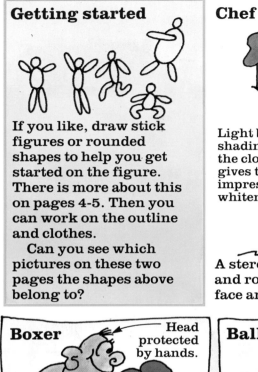

If you like, draw stick figures or rounded shapes to help you get started on the figure. There is more about this on pages 4-5. Then you can work on the outline and clothes.

Can you see which pictures on these two pages the shapes above belong to?

There is more about this on pages 4-5.

Chef

Chef's hat

Light blue shading on the clothes gives the impression of whiteness.

A stereotyped chef is jolly and round, with a big red face and a moustache.

Burglar

Loot bag

LOOT

Striped jersey

Flashlight

The burglar creeps along on tip-toe.

No real burglar would wear this kind of outfit, but this is how they are often drawn in cartoons.

Boxer

Head protected by hands.

Opponent knocked out.

The boxer is muscular and heavy, with a squashy nose and swollen ear. He wears big gloves and laced boots.

Ballerina

These lines show she is pirouetting.

Slender limbs and hands.

The ballerina is very slim and light on her feet. She stands on her toes.

Spy

The spy's hat is pulled down and the collar of his coat is turned up. One furtive eye looks out from under the brim of his hat.

Pop star

A pop star wears trendy clothes and jewelry. Draw her mouth open and colored lights behind her.

Soccer player

A soccer player looks fit and energetic. You can draw him wearing your favorite team's strip.

Jockey

Jodphurs

Riding crop

A jockey is small, wiry and bow-legged. He wears a peaked hat with the brim turned up and racing colors on his clothes.

Gangster

Dark glasses

A gangster wears smart clothes, smokes a cigar and carries a violin case to conceal his gun.

More stereotypes

Clown

Fairytale princess

Cowboy

Witch

Butler

Here are some ideas for some more stereotypes. Can you think of others?

Cartoons growing up

As people grow older, their bodies change shape. So does the way they stand, sit and move.

These pages show some of the tricks involved in drawing people of different ages.

Babies

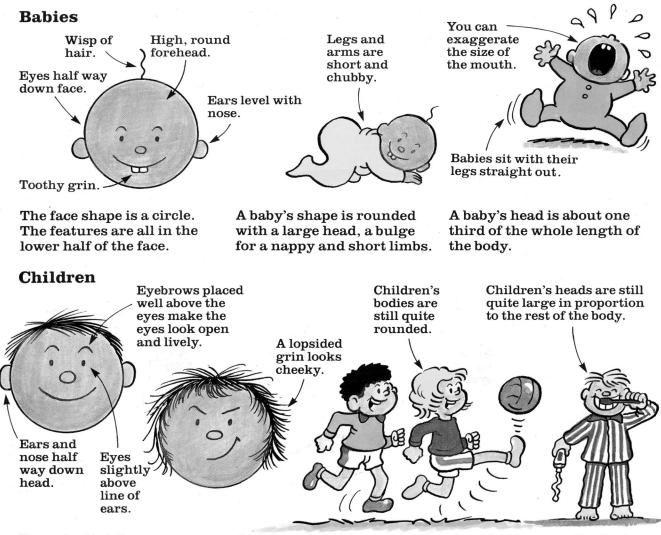

Wisp of hair.

High, round forehead.

Eyes half way down face.

Ears level with nose.

Toothy grin.

Legs and arms are short and chubby.

You can exaggerate the size of the mouth.

Babies sit with their legs straight out.

The face shape is a circle. The features are all in the lower half of the face.

A baby's shape is rounded with a large head, a bulge for a nappy and short limbs.

A baby's head is about one third of the whole length of the body.

Children

Eyebrows placed well above the eyes make the eyes look open and lively.

A lopsided grin looks cheeky.

Children's bodies are still quite rounded.

Children's heads are still quite large in proportion to the rest of the body.

Ears and nose half way down head.

Eyes slightly above line of ears.

There is slightly more space between the chin and mouth on a child than on a baby.

Girls' and boys' faces are similar shapes but they can have different hairstyles.

As a child grows, the limbs get longer in proportion to the rest of the body.

Men and women

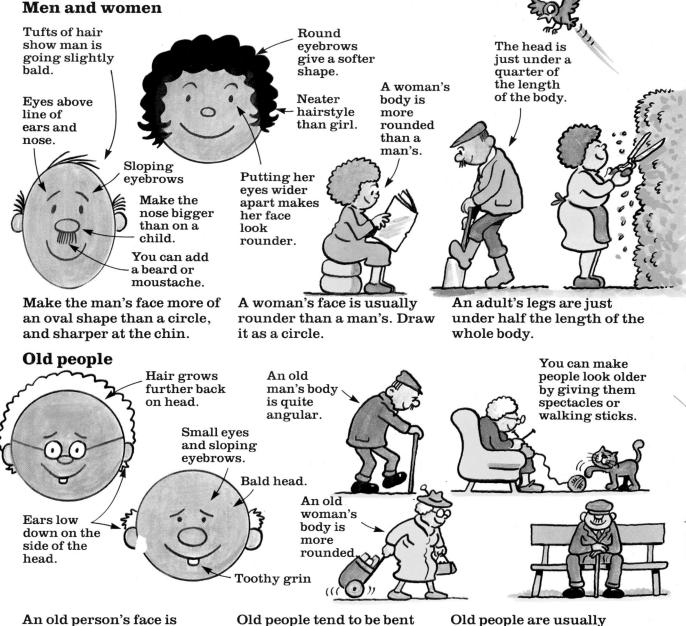

Tufts of hair show man is going slightly bald.

Eyes above line of ears and nose.

Round eyebrows give a softer shape.

Neater hairstyle than girl.

A woman's body is more rounded than a man's.

The head is just under a quarter of the length of the body.

Sloping eyebrows

Make the nose bigger than on a child.

You can add a beard or moustache.

Putting her eyes wider apart makes her face look rounder.

Make the man's face more of an oval shape than a circle, and sharper at the chin.

A woman's face is usually rounder than a man's. Draw it as a circle.

An adult's legs are just under half the length of the whole body.

Old people

Hair grows further back on head.

An old man's body is quite angular.

You can make people look older by giving them spectacles or walking sticks.

Small eyes and sloping eyebrows.

Bald head.

Ears low down on the side of the head.

An old woman's body is more rounded.

Toothy grin

An old person's face is round, like a baby's. It has other similar features.

Old people tend to be bent over. Their heads are placed further forwards.

Old people are usually smaller and more fragile than younger adults.

19

Scenery and perspective

Scenery and backgrounds can add a lot of information about what is happening in your pictures. You need to keep the scenery quite simple, though, so that characters stand out against it.

Here, you can see how to get a sense of distance, or depth, into pictures. This is called drawing in perspective.

Tricks of perspective

The further away something is, the smaller it looks. The woman in this picture is drawn smaller than the burglar to make her look further away.

Draw the woman further up the picture than the burglar. Otherwise it will look like the picture above. She just looks like a tiny person.

Parallel lines appear to get closer the further away they are. They seem to meet on the horizon. This point is called the vanishing point.

A high vanishing point makes it seem as if you are looking down on the picture. What happens if you draw a low vanishing point?

Fence posts get closer together.

Pavement and fence get narrower.

A picture in perspective

Here is a picture in perspective. The woman is drawn smaller and further up than the burglar to make her look further away.

If the vanishing point falls outside your picture area, try sketching it in pencil as above. This helps to get all the lines properly in perspective. You can erase the lines later.

Adding depth

Lines going across a picture can also add depth. Here, the lines of hills make it look as if the scenery goes back for miles.

See how the road gets narrower in perspective as it gets further away, and the birds get smaller.

Scenery gets paler and less distinct the further away it is.

The man is large because he is nearest to you.

◄ In this picture, the curved lines of the circus arena show the depth of the picture.
Color and shape are less distinct the further away they are, so only the front row of people are drawn in. Colored blobs suggest the rest of the crowd.

Drawing objects

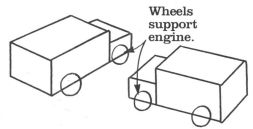

Wheels support engine.

Erase these lines.

Square or oblong objects, such as tables and chairs, are quite easy to draw in perspective. The opposite sides are almost parallel.

You can draw a more complicated object, such as a car, by first constructing it out of a number of box shapes.

Then round off the corners and add the details. You may need to practice this a bit. Looking at an object while you draw it can help.

Cartoon jokes

Cartoon jokes are often printed in black and white in newspapers and magazines. They may be in the form of a strip (see pages 24-25) or a single picture, called a single cartoon. The one on the right is a single cartoon.

Here you can find out what kind of jokes make good cartoons, what materials cartoonists use and some tips on drawing single cartoons yourself.

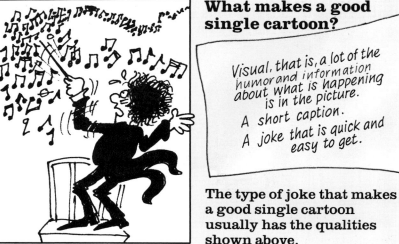

What makes a good single cartoon?

Visual, that is, a lot of the humor and information about what is happening is in the picture.
A short caption.
A joke that is quick and easy to get.

The type of joke that makes a good single cartoon usually has the qualities shown above.

Ideas for jokes

It can be difficult to think up ideas for jokes on the spot. It helps to think first of a theme or situation. This may then suggest something funny to you.

Here are some common cartoon themes and some jokes based on them.

A desert island

This is probably the most common theme for single cartoon jokes.

A hospital

GET YOUR ACCIDENT INSURANCE HERE →

This joke has two common cartoon themes – hospitals and manhole covers.

Vampires

This is funny because it shows a monstrous creature doing something ordinary.

Materials you can use

The materials shown below are enough to get you started. You may already have them. If you like, though, you can buy the more specialized materials shown on the rest of this page.

Hard   Medium   Soft

Pencils are marked to show how hard or soft they are. Experiment to find a type you like. Pencils range from 9B (very soft) to 9H (very hard).

You can draw on good quality typing paper which is quite cheap.

Fiber tip pens do not smudge or blot. In time, though, the ink fades in daylight. If you find it easier, sketch a drawing in pencil first and then ink over it. You can cover mistakes with typewriter correction fluid.

How professional cartoonists work

Single cartoons are drawn in black and white for printing in newspapers and magazines. Here are some of the materials that cartoonists use. You could try some of them yourself.

Pencils. The artist might use a medium pencil for outlines and a softer one for shading.

Fine paintbrushes

Art board. This can have different surfaces from very smooth and shiny to quite rough and soft.

Fiber tip pens

Drawing pens. These come with different thicknesses of nib. They draw a very even line.

Dip pens and Indian ink. You can get different shapes and thicknesses of nib.

Cartridge paper takes pens, pencils or paint equally well.

Fountain pens

Cartoons are mostly printed quite small. They are usually drawn larger than final size and reduced photographically before printing.

The cartoonist is told what size the cartoon will be printed.

By drawing a diagonal line across a box that size, the artist can scale the size up so that it is larger but still the same shape.

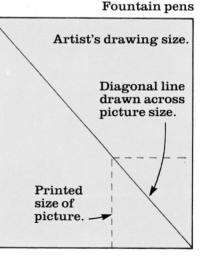

Artist's drawing size.

Diagonal line drawn across picture size.

Printed size of picture.

Strip cartoons

A strip cartoon is a joke told in more than one frame. Like a single cartoon, the joke needs to be visual. It can be like a short story with a punchline.

One of the hardest things about drawing a strip cartoon is making characters look the same in each frame. To start with, only use one or two characters. Give them features which you find easy to draw.

How to start

As with single cartoons, think of a theme first and make up a joke around it.

Close-ups varied with larger scenes.

Divide the joke up into three or four stages. You can vary the sizes of the frames, and close-ups with larger scenes, to make the strip look more interesting.

Speech bubbles

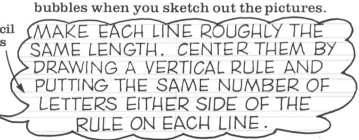

Put bubbles over background areas with no detail.

You can put speech and thoughts in bubbles in the pictures. These can be different shapes. The shape of the bubble may suggest the way something is being said.

Keep the speech short or the strip gets complicated and the bubbles take up too much room. Make sure you allow room for bubbles when you sketch out the pictures.

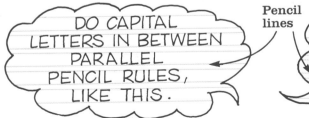

Pencil lines

DO CAPITAL LETTERS IN BETWEEN PARALLEL PENCIL RULES, LIKE THIS.

MAKE EACH LINE ROUGHLY THE SAME LENGTH. CENTER THEM BY DRAWING A VERTICAL RULE AND PUTTING THE SAME NUMBER OF LETTERS EITHER SIDE OF THE RULE ON EACH LINE.

It is best to do the lettering before you draw the bubble outline. Use a pen with a fine tip.

To get the letters the same height, draw parallel pencil lines and letter in between them, as above. Then erase the pencil lines. The letters are likely to be quite small, so it is best to use capital letters which are easier to read.

A finished strip

This strip is about a caveman. He is quite an easy character to repeat from frame to frame because of his simple features and clothing.*

Speech bubble over the sky area.

Different sized frames make strip more interesting.

Sound effects make the strip more fun. As you read it you imagine the noises so it is a bit like watching a film.

Bright colors make the characters stand out. The background is paler.

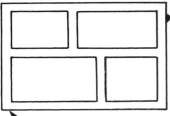

A lot of the humor in a strip cartoon comes from the expressions on the characters faces.

When positioning speech bubbles, remember that people read from left to right down the frame. They will read bubbles at the top before they read bubbles further down.

Borders for the strip

Border round strip.

Use a ruler and a pen with a slightly thicker tip than the one you used for the lettering. You can put the whole strip in a larger box.

Freehand borders are finished off without a ruler.

1. Place a ruler just below where you want to draw the line.

2. Run your fingers along the ruler as you paint. (You may need to practice this.)

The borders round the frames can make a strip look neat and tidy or free and artistic. Here are some ideas for different borders.

Freehand borders give a sketchy effect. To keep them straight, draw the lines in pencil with a ruler. Then go over them in ink.

Paintbrush borders are nice because the line varies slightly in thickness. You can get a straight line using the method above.

*You can find out how to draw dinosaurs on pages 46-47.

Comic strips

You may have your own favorite comics. The stories in them are fun to read because there is very little text and a lot of action in the pictures.

These two pages describe how a comic strip artist creates a comic strip. You could try making up your own comic strip in the same way.

Creating a comic strip

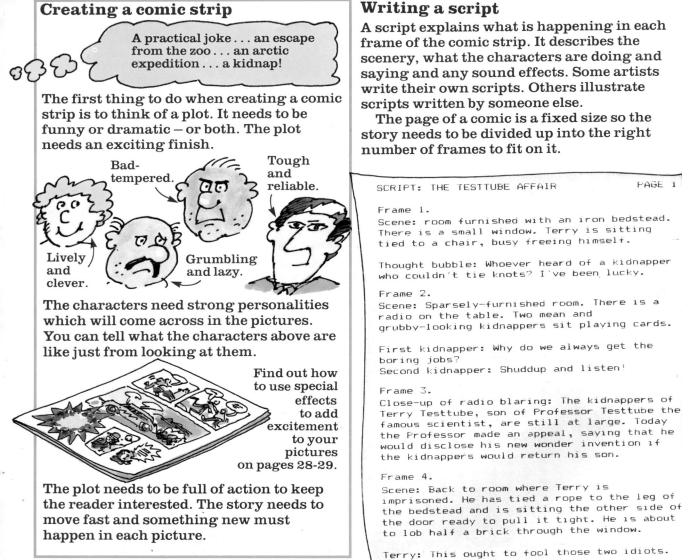

A practical joke ... an escape from the zoo ... an arctic expedition ... a kidnap!

The first thing to do when creating a comic strip is to think of a plot. It needs to be funny or dramatic — or both. The plot needs an exciting finish.

Bad-tempered.

Tough and reliable.

Lively and clever.

Grumbling and lazy.

The characters need strong personalities which will come across in the pictures. You can tell what the characters above are like just from looking at them.

Find out how to use special effects to add excitement to your pictures on pages 28-29.

The plot needs to be full of action to keep the reader interested. The story needs to move fast and something new must happen in each picture.

Writing a script

A script explains what is happening in each frame of the comic strip. It describes the scenery, what the characters are doing and saying and any sound effects. Some artists write their own scripts. Others illustrate scripts written by someone else.

The page of a comic is a fixed size so the story needs to be divided up into the right number of frames to fit on it.

SCRIPT: THE TESTTUBE AFFAIR   PAGE 1

Frame 1.
Scene: room furnished with an iron bedstead. There is a small window. Terry is sitting tied to a chair, busy freeing himself.

Thought bubble: Whoever heard of a kidnapper who couldn't tie knots? I've been lucky.

Frame 2.
Scene: Sparsely-furnished room. There is a radio on the table. Two mean and grubby-looking kidnappers sit playing cards.

First kidnapper: Why do we always get the boring jobs?
Second kidnapper: Shuddup and listen!

Frame 3.
Close-up of radio blaring: The kidnappers of Terry Testtube, son of Professor Testtube the famous scientist, are still at large. Today the Professor made an appeal, saying that he would disclose his new wonder invention if the kidnappers would return his son.

Frame 4.
Scene: Back to room where Terry is imprisoned. He has tied a rope to the leg of the bedstead and is sitting the other side of the door ready to pull it tight. He is about to lob half a brick through the window.

Terry: This ought to fool those two idiots.

Drawing the strip

Here you can see how the script on the left (you can only see the first page) was made into a finished comic strip. It was drawn using a dip pen with a sprung nib. The nib gives a varying thickness of line depending on how hard it is pressed.

The story is mainly told in the pictures but there are bubbles for speech and thoughts.

Pressure on nib gives a thick line.

Frame sizes are varied to make strip more interesting.

A line of text at the top can explain changes of scene or time lapses.

Some frames can be left without borders to add variety.

Light pressure on nib gives a finer line.

This is a freeze-frame picture (see page 15).

Scenery can make the strip come to life.

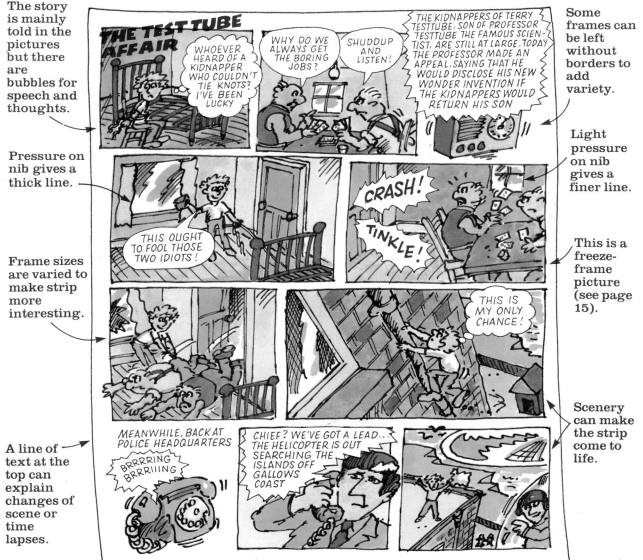

Special effects

Special effects can make cartoons look exciting. Here are some ideas for how to add drama and atmosphere to your pictures. You can make them spooky, mysterious, shocking or scary. You can also find out how to add sound effects.

Sound effects

You can add sound effects by using words and shapes which suggest the sound. The most common ones are explosions but there are lots of others you can use.

Jagged speech bubble suggests shock.

Shadows and silhouettes

Using different lighting effects for night pictures can make them look creepy or mysterious. Here are some suggestions:

Silhouettes in a lighted window. These are made by people sitting in front of a source of light.

Huge shadow on wall.

Silhouette of a castle in a thunderstorm.

28

Scary effects

This picture uses the effect of a harmless tree that looks scary in the dark. You could try a similar picture using a hat and coat hanging up to look like a sinister person.

Lines suggesting speed.

This type of shading, where you use lots of lines close together, is called hatching.*

Two strip cartoons

These strip cartoons use some of the special effects described on these pages.

A strip cartoon to try

Here is a script for a strip cartoon involving special effects for you to try.
Frame 1: Silhouettes of people by a bonfire.
Frame 2: Boy dressed up as a ghost frightens them away.

Frame 3: Boy takes sheet off and is shocked to hear laughter coming from a spooky tree silhouette.
Sound effect: HO HO HO

You can find out about other ways to shade on page 71.

Comic books

Comic books are like long comic strips. The story is told in pictures with lots of action and excitement.

Tintin is one of the best known comic book characters. He and his dog, Snowy, first appeared in 1929 as a comic strip serial in a weekly children's newspaper. Later, the stories were made into magazines and books.

Who created Tintin?

Tintin

Snowy

Professor Calculus

Captain Haddock

Characters in the Tintin stories.*

One of the identical twin detectives, Thomson and Thompson.

A Belgian man called Hergé created Tintin. Hergé's real name was Georges Remi. The name Hergé came from the French pronunciation of his initials, G.R., backwards. He was born in 1907 and died in 1983.

The Studios Hergé

Until the early 1940s, Hergé worked alone on Tintin. Later he assembled a team to help color in the pictures, letter the speech bubbles and so on. This team became known as the Studios Hergé. All the stories were thoroughly researched so that details of costume, architecture, machinery and so on were correct.

The ship Unicorn, from *The Secret of the Unicorn* and *Red Rackham's Treasure* was based on ships in the French navy in the 17th century.*

The Inca masks in this picture from *Prisoners of the Sun*, were based on the sketch on the right.*

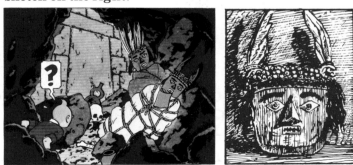

Sketch by a 19th century explorer of Peru and Bolivia.

First Hergé wrote a plot and sketched the drawings. He then worked on the drawings, redrawing them as many as ten times. The drawings were then handed to his assistants. They filled in backgrounds, colored the pictures and drew and lettered the speech bubbles. Hergé drew all the characters and checked the final pictures.

Hergé's techniques

The Tintin books have a very distinctive style. Here you can see some of its features in a section from *Prisoners of the Sun*.

Many of them add variety to the picture strips so that they look lively, exciting and never boring.*

Unusual angles look dramatic and make the story more interesting.

The pictures are clear and the outlines are unbroken.

Hergé varied the sizes of frames to add variety and suit the picture.

The faces show many different expressions.

Colors are clear and flat with no shading.

Costumes and scenery were thoroughly researched so that all details were correct.

Background colors are plain and muted. The bright costumes stand out against them.

Hergé varied close-ups with larger pictures of single characters and scenes with lots of people.

The stories are full of suspense and drama. This is because they were first published in newspaper serials. Hergé needed to create suspense at the end of each instalment.

*Drawings by Hergé. © Studios Hergé/Casterman Publishers

Drawing animals

You can draw animals in a similar way to drawing people, by using simple shapes and lines and adding features.

Animals make good cartoons because you can use their natural characteristics, such as claws, tails, ears and so on to give them personality. Here are lots of animals to draw.

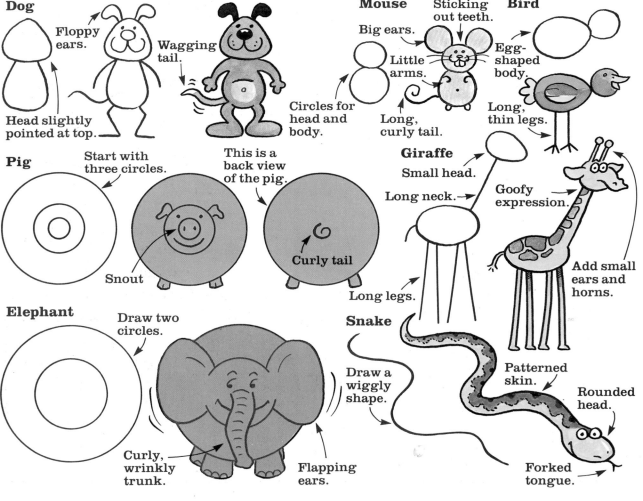

Cat

Round head.

Egg-shaped body.

Add face, ears and sticks for arms and legs.

Dog

Floppy ears.

Wagging tail.

Head slightly pointed at top.

Pig

Start with three circles.

Snout

This is a back view of the pig.

Curly tail

Elephant

Draw two circles.

Curly, wrinkly trunk.

Flapping ears.

Mouse

Big ears.

Little arms.

Sticking out teeth.

Circles for head and body.

Long, curly tail.

Bird

Egg-shaped body.

Long, thin legs.

Giraffe

Small head.

Long neck.

Goofy expression.

Long legs.

Add small ears and horns.

Snake

Draw a wiggly shape.

Patterned skin.

Rounded head.

Forked tongue.

Lion

Body shape is similar to dog.

Curly mane.

Snout

Large paws.

Eyebrows raised in a superior expression.

Fish

Round eyes.

Gaping mouth.

Tropical fish.

Monkey

Sticking out ears.

Long arms.

Similar body shape to cat with snout.

Thin legs.

Long tail.

Whale

Rounded fish shape.

Water spout.

Cow

Triangular-shaped head.

Oblong-shaped body.

Udder

Horns and ears.

Sheep

Large body.

Small head.

Silly expression.

Woolly fleece.

Thin legs.

Animals in cartoons

Cartoons may look very violent but usually no real harm is done. The cartoon below might help you think up a few of your own animal cartoons.

How cartoon films are made

The most famous cartoon film maker in the world was Walt Disney. He made such films as Mickey Mouse and Bambi. He started work in the 1920s. Although equipment and materials have improved over the years, the way cartoon films are made has changed very little.

On the next four pages you can find out how cartoon films are made. This is called cartoon animation.

How film works

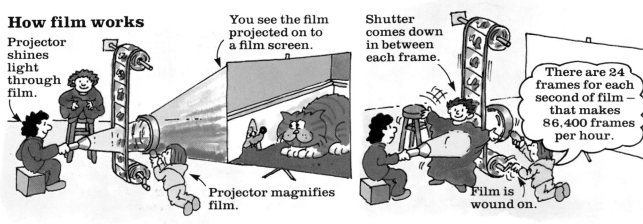

Projector shines light through film.

You see the film projected on to a film screen.

Projector magnifies film.

Shutter comes down in between each frame.

Film is wound on.

There are 24 frames for each second of film — that makes 86,400 frames per hour.

A film is a sequence of tiny pictures, or frames. There are 24 frames for each second of film. A projector shines light through them and magnifies them.

Each frame is held still in front of the projector just long enough for you to see it. Then a shutter comes down while the next frame is positioned.

This happens so fast that you do not notice individual frames or the shutter. Without the shutter between frames, the film would look like a long blur.

Making the film

A cartoon film is made by taking photos of thousands of drawings. The drawings show all the different stages of movement.

The photos of the drawings are combined into a film strip. (There is more about how all this is done over the page.)

Each photo makes one frame. 24 frames make one second of the film. Below, you can see the frames in one second of a film.

24 frames make one second of film.

Planning the film

The story of the film is divided up into scenes. The artists working on the film, called the animators, do a set of drawings. This shows what happens in each scene. It is called a storyboard.

The storyboard is a bit like a strip cartoon. What the characters are saying is written under the pictures.

Storyboard ↗

Animating the film

The animators break each scene down into different movements. Then, each animator works on drawing one movement at a time: for instance, a sneeze.

The animator draws the start and end of the sneeze and a few of the main stages in between.

These pictures are called extremes. Each extreme is numbered. The numbers show how many other stages need to be drawn in between to complete the sneeze.

Extremes

The animator has a chart showing what will happen during each split second of the film — action, speech, sound effects and music. The movements drawn are matched to the sound.

Chart

Turn the page to see what happens next.

Completing the drawings

Extreme

In-betweener adds these pictures.

Extreme

Once all the extremes have been drawn, they are passed on to other members of the animating team.

These members are called in-betweeners because they do the drawings in between the extremes.

The numbers on the extremes show the in-betweener how many more pictures are needed.

How the artists work

Each animator or in-betweener works on a flat box with a glass surface, called a light box.

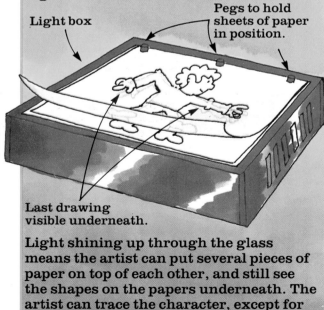

Light box

Pegs to hold sheets of paper in position.

Last drawing visible underneath.

Light shining up through the glass means the artist can put several pieces of paper on top of each other, and still see the shapes on the papers underneath. The artist can trace the character, except for parts that are meant to move.

Ink and paint

The finished drawings are traced on to transparent sheets called cels.

Each cel is then turned over and painted on the back, so that brush strokes do not show on the front. The cels are now ready for the next stage, when they are photographed. This stage is called shooting.

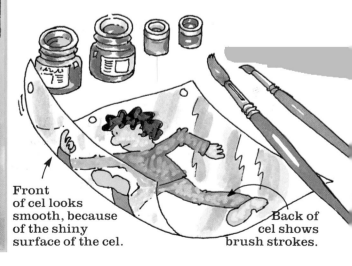

Front of cel looks smooth, because of the shiny surface of the cel.

Back of cel shows brush strokes.

Background scenery

Background scenery is painted on long rolls of paper. During shooting, the scenery is laid on the plate of a cartoon camera (see right). The cel with the character drawn on it is placed on top of it.

Background scenery

Cel with character drawn on it.

Each time a new cel is put on the plate, the background scenery can be moved to either side. This makes it look as if the character is moving.

Background scenery rolls this way.

The character stays in the same place on the plate of the camera, but the scenery is moved behind him. This makes it look as if he is running along.

Cartoon camera

The type of camera used to take photographs for a cartoon film is called a cartoon camera. One cel at a time is placed on the plate of the camera and a picture taken. All the photos are combined into one reel of film.

Cartoon camera plate.

Flick the pages and watch your cartoon say hello.

Animate your own cartoon

Use a small notebook with thin paper so you can see the line of a black felt tip pen through the page.

Hold the notebook firmly closed. Draw three thick, black lines across the tops of all the pages.

On the first page, copy the picture above. Tear it out. Number the next ten pages from one to ten.

Trace your picture on to pages one and ten. Use the marks at the top of the page to line the pages up.

On page five, trace the head, but make him raise his hat. You now have three key pictures.

Draw the in-between stages. Start with page nine and work back. Trace parts staying still.

Mix and match

Here are lots of pictures of heads, bodies and legs from different sides. You can copy them and use them in your own pictures. Remember that a person's head might be facing you while the body is sideways, and vice versa.

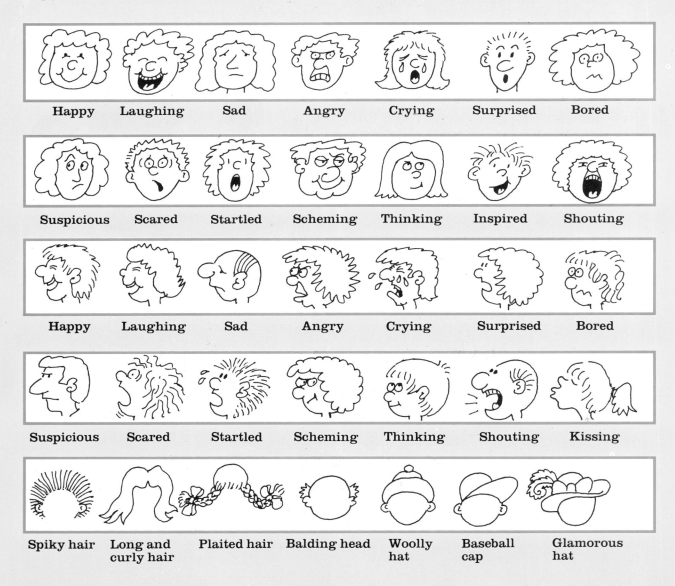

Happy　　Laughing　　Sad　　Angry　　Crying　　Surprised　　Bored

Suspicious　　Scared　　Startled　　Scheming　　Thinking　　Inspired　　Shouting

Happy　　Laughing　　Sad　　Angry　　Crying　　Surprised　　Bored

Suspicious　　Scared　　Startled　　Scheming　　Thinking　　Shouting　　Kissing

Spiky hair　　Long and curly hair　　Plaited hair　　Balding head　　Woolly hat　　Baseball cap　　Glamorous hat

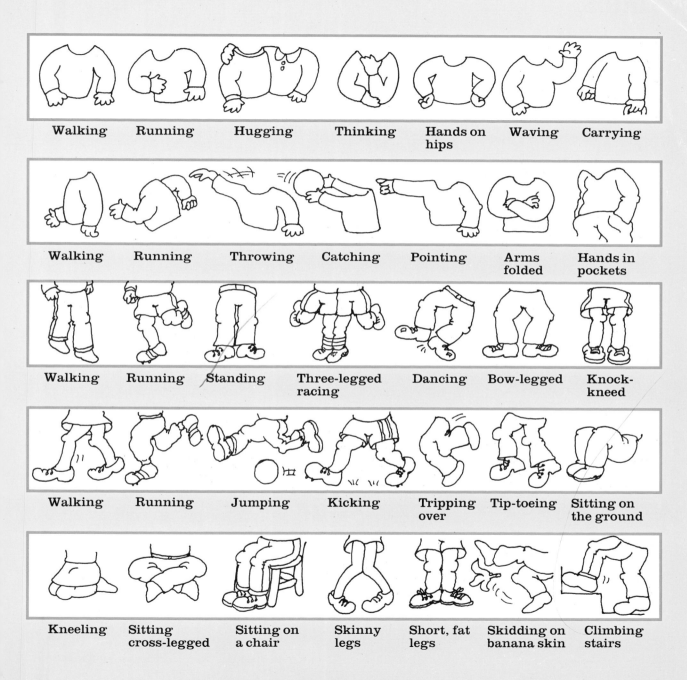

Walking   Running   Hugging   Thinking   Hands on   Waving   Carrying
                                              hips

Walking   Running   Throwing   Catching   Pointing   Arms   Hands in
                                                           folded   pockets

Walking   Running   Standing   Three-legged   Dancing   Bow-legged   Knock-
                                  racing   kneed

Walking   Running   Jumping   Kicking   Tripping   Tip-toeing   Sitting on
                                            over   the ground

Kneeling   Sitting   Sitting on   Skinny   Short, fat   Skidding on   Climbing
            cross-legged   a chair   legs   legs   banana skin   stairs

Index

First published in 1987 by Usborne Publishing Ltd,
Usborne House, 83–85 Saffron Hill, London EC1N 8RT, England.

Copyright © Usborne Publishing Ltd. 1987

The name Usborne and the device 🐝 are Trade Marks of
Usborne Publishing Ltd.

Printed in Great Britain.   **American edition 1987.**